Winnie-the-Pooh

The Great Heffalump Hunt

Giles Andreae

For Vic, Flinn, Freya, Nat and Jackson, with love, G.A.

EGMONT
We bring stories to life

First published in Great Britain 2017 by Egmont UK Limited
The Yellow Building, 1 Nicholas Road, London, W11 4AN
www.egmont.co.uk

Written by Giles Andreae.
Illustrations by Angela Rozelaar, Eleanor Taylor and Mikki Butterley.

Based on the 'Winnie-the-Pooh' works by A.A.Milne and E.H.Shepard
Copyright © Disney Enterprises Inc. 2017

ISBN 978 1 4052 7830 0
60936/2
Printed in Malaysia

Winnie-the-Pooh
The Great Heffalump Hunt

Giles Andreae

Piglet trotted happily
Beside his best friend Pooh,
Talking about nothing much,
As best **friends**
often do.

When suddenly Pooh stopped and said,
"I've got a Grand Idea,
I'm going to catch a **Heffalump.**
I've heard they live round here."

"A **Heffalump!**" squeaked Piglet,
"But they're huge, wild, scary beasts.
And Rabbit says they like to roast
Fresh Piglets for their feasts!"

"Well, that's why I must catch one!"
Pooh declared. Then, with a clap,
He said, "Aha! I've got a plan ...
Let's set a **Cunning Trap!**"

"Now, what might **hungry Heffalumps** Find tempting as a treat? Aside from Piglets," pondered Pooh, "My guess is ... something **sweet**."

"A **yumptious** jar of **honey**, then!" Said Piglet with a grin. "We'll bait a trap with honey And he'll simply fall right in!"

"What a
Grand Idea!"
said Pooh,
"Let's do it now - tonight!

I'll go and fetch some **honey**
While you dig a pit,
alright?"

Pooh went and got the **honey,**
But before he reached the pit,
A little voice inside him said,
"Just taste a **tiny bit.**"

He found the pit his friend had dug
And passed the **honey** down.
"There's hardly any left!" squeaked Piglet,
Giving Pooh a **frown**.

"There's just the right amount," said Pooh,
"I gave it **careful** thought.
Let's meet at **six tomorrow** then
And find out what we've caught!"

So Pooh and Piglet went to bed,
But neither was prepared
For the fact that Pooh was **hungry...**

And that Piglet was, well...
scared.

"That jar of honey in our trap,"
Groaned Pooh, "it was my last.
Oh bother! Double bother!
And, if no-one's listening,
BLAST!

Just **one more** little pawful
Would be neither here nor there.
A **Heffalump** who's hungry
Wouldn't notice ... wouldn't care."

So he set off through the **forest**
With the moonlight overhead ...

And, at that moment, Piglet sat up,
Wide awake in bed.

"That **horrid, hairy Heffalump,**
He might not like Pooh's honey!
Ohhh ... what if all he wants
Is **juicy Piglets** in his tummy?

But Pooh will be there with me,"
Piglet thought, "my **best friend,** Pooh.
It's **scary** when you're one,
But it's much **friendlier** with **two.**"

So just before his clock struck six,
He **tiptoed** out the door.
The leaves and branches crackled
On the **frosty** forest floor.

Then suddenly he heard a noise
That chilled him to the bone.
A ghostly wail, a growl, a roar,
A mournful, muffled moan.

"Where are you, Pooh?" called Piglet.
His **heart** beat fast with dread.
"I'm in the pit!" he heard Pooh cry,
"And something's got my **head!**"

"The Heffalump!
squeaked Piglet.
"It's in the pit with Pooh,
And I'm much too small to help him
Oh, there's nothing I can do!"

But something in his little soul
Prevented him from running,
And Piglet's voice rose clear and strong,
"Hold on, Pooh Bear ...
I'M COMING!"

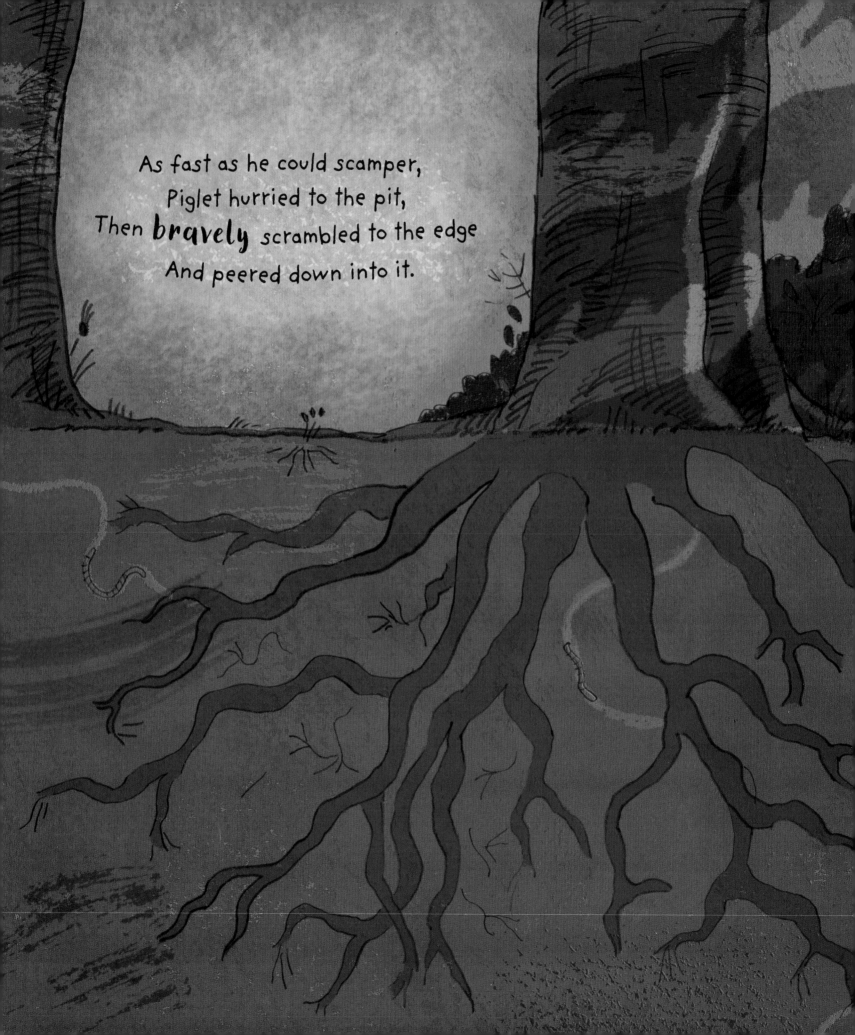

As fast as he could scamper,
Piglet hurried to the pit,
Then **bravely** scrambled to the edge
And peered down into it.

"A **Heffalump!** It's got him!
And it's shaking him about!"
And all that Piglet saw
Was Pooh's poor bottom sticking out.

He summoned all his strength
And smacked the monster on the head.
"Take that, you naughty
Heffalump!
Now, let Pooh go!" he said.

Then Piglet gave
one final heave
And, with a squelching sound,

Out popped Pooh completely
And collapsed
onto the ground.

"The **Heffalump!** It's vanished!"
Piglet said, "It won't get far!"
But there, in Piglet's arms,
Pooh saw ... an **empty honey jar.**

"The **Heffalump!**" said Pooh,
"Um, yes, I'm pretty sure he's gone.
I thought I saw him too
But, Piglet ... maybe we were wrong.

You see, I got quite **hungry**
When I went to have my nap,
But the only snack I knew of
Was the one inside this trap.

I took a lick. My head got stuck.
I thought, 'this is the end!'
But there you were, dear Piglet,
My brave rescuer. My friend!"

"I did it," Piglet slowly spoke,
"Because I love you, Pooh,
And I know, if it were me,
That you would do the same thing too."

"I would," said Pooh,
"And thank you."
Then he sniffed and wiped his eye.
"I'd rescue you from
Heffalumps,
But maybe ... let's not try."

"We're lucky, Pooh," said Piglet

As they set off home together,

"That you and I are such good friends."

"Best friends," said Pooh ...

"...FOREVER."